The Nanny Diaries

#2

Vicki Sweet

Printed in the United States of America

IMDB: 9781952422119
First Printing, 2020

DarlingCoxx@gmail.com
Instagram: @DarlingCoxx
OnlyFans: @DarlingCoxx

Chapter One

Dear Diary,

When the Rayburn's took out the ad for a live-in nanny, they lied. It was advertised as needing a caretaker for two elementary age children because their parents worked second shift. Their father, Lance, works second shift as a police officer. Their mother? The only work she does is maintaining her looks and running around behind his back.

Lance married into money. Tori's parents are loaded, and give her whatever she asks for including their house. That's not including the trust funds they set up for her.

At first, I wondered why Lance even worked. I figured he must really enjoy what he does to keep doing it when he doesn't have to. I mean if I was set like that, I wouldn't work. I'm starting to suspect he goes to work to have a break from his wife.

Anyway, they told me during my interview that they worked late hours. They needed someone to get the children off to school in the mornings. After school, I'd be responsible for getting them home or to practices, and to make sure they did their homework. I'd also have to prepare a meal for the family for dinner. I'd be allowed to eat with them of course. It sounded pretty simple and easy. The money was good, so why not? I didn't realize I'd be running after the children all evening while Tori leered at me from a distance because they were interrupting her as she made plans for a new dick to suck.

I've been here for two weeks. This is what I've learned. Tori doesn't work. She doesn't even do volunteer work like how most of the elite wives in town busy themselves. All this woman does is shop and cheat on her husband. Oh, that's when she's not being a bitch to me for no reason. As the days pass, her attitude toward me gets worse. She's the one who insisted on the nanny!

Lance is pretty decent. He doesn't say much. He gets home

close to midnight, but it varies. When he comes home, his routine is the same. He changes out of his uniform, relaxes for a bit with a drink or two, and then heads to bed. He wakes up around noon, and most of the time, I don't see him before he leaves for work. I just hear him moving around.

It was explained to me that I would have the days mostly to myself unless the children were home. What a crock of shit. The first day, yeah. It went off without a hitch. It was Lance's day off. They wanted me to start on a day when he was home. Fine. I didn't think nothing of it at the time. He was helping me find where everything was kept in the kitchen, so I could make dinner. We bumped heads after standing up from the cabinet we were searching through at the same time and laughed. Typhoon Tori came running in demanding to know why we were acting so buddy-buddy! He's barely spoke to me since, except for the next night when Tori caused all the drama.

The real reason they wanted me to start on his day off? Tori doesn't do jack shit around this place. I would be surprised if she knew where the coffee was kept, but heaven help us if it's not brewed for her in the afternoon when she finally drags her ass out of bed. I think she couldn't be bothered with helping me both because she's a selfish, lazy piece of trash and because she doesn't know how to do a damn a thing in the first place.

So as I was saying, the first day went alright. On day two, Lance had to work. As soon as Tori's entitled, spoiled ass got out of bed around two, she was demanding to know why I hadn't started the laundry yet! Uh, maybe because you didn't hire me to be your maid. That night she was on Lance as soon as he walked in the door. After a heated argument, Lance offered me more money to take care of the house as well.

It's not that I was eavesdropping. They had the fight right in front of me. That's when I learned the reason I was hired. Tori couldn't be bothered to raise her own children, and she was mad Lance insisted on keeping his job when there was no need. If he wanted to work, he had to hire help. That's what he did. That night, he told her if she didn't want to take care of the house that she repeatedly reminded him was hers, she could pay for the maid.

Way to go, Lance. You should stand up for yourself more often.

That's how I got roped into housekeeping duties. My pay was doubled. Each week, he pays me for caring for the children, and she pays me for cleaning. It works except it triggered her attitude toward me.

Night three, Lance went to work. I cooked dinner. It was on the dining room table, and I was about to take my seat with the family when Tori announced I could eat in the kitchen. She wasn't even eating with us! She just marched in the room to kick me out of it. Fine. No sweat off my back.

But come the next night that Lance was off? Oh, then I was welcome to eat with the family. When I went to sit at the kitchen island, Lance looked mortified and asked what I was doing. He moved me back to the dining room immediately. Tori shot me daggered looks, telling me with her eyes if I opened my mouth and said a word, I'd be packing my bags.

Lance has never wronged me except he should put his wife in

check more often. It doesn't take a rocket scientist to figure out he's simply chasing her family's money. Tori holds divorce over his head like it's nothing. I've heard her complain to her friends that she's worried her Catholic parents would cut her off if she divorces him without good cause, so I know it's all for effect. Lance must not be clued in to that. She only needs to mention the "D" word, and he falls over himself to kiss her ass and get back in her good graces. It's sickening. They deserve each other really.

That's the game we play now. When Lance is home, Tori treats me... Well, she's still a bitch, but better than the usual subhuman treatment I get from her. Luckily, she's not home a lot, so I don't deal with it constantly. Two can play at this game. The night she first sent me to the kitchen with my plate I decided come hell or high water, I was going to fuck her husband.

I've been biding my time, learning their routines. Nothing can stop a woman on a mission. Sure I may be young, but it doesn't matter that I'm only twenty-one. Being a bitch is ingrained in a female's DNA. You don't want to be on the receiving end of our wrath. We don't always come at you head on with our fists high. Sometimes, our payback takes careful planning, and it's so much sweeter to watch it play out.

I've divided my plan into phases. Tonight I started phase one. It's a simple one really. I need to get better acquainted with Lance. We need to become friendly. By that, I mean I need him to notice me and put the thought of fucking me in his head. Sure, it'll be a harmless fantasy at first, but as time goes on, I'll make sure he's picturing me when his wife is giving him a pity fuck to shut him up about not getting laid for a while. I'm usually in bed when he gets home, but not necessarily asleep. Tori is almost always gone at that time. Out with "friends" who happen to be men with hard cocks she can't seem to suck enough. Most nights, I'd have the chance for a few moments alone with him.

After the children were asleep, I dug out the sexiest nightie I owned. It's not something I would usually wear here, but it was necessary tonight. Its skin tight black lace that shows every curve and most of my breasts are visible through the thin material. It's so short that it barely covers my ass. Any movement at all, and it starts riding up. It's not the type of garment that's meant to be worn for long. As soon as I heard the car pull into the driveway, I raced down to the bathroom off the kitchen. Lance's first stop when he walks through the backdoor is to drop his keys, wallet and so forth in the basket on the counter near the door before heading upstairs to his room to change.

Standing at the door of the bathroom, I waited until I heard his footsteps just about to pass by then I stepped out. The look on his face! I apologized profusely and waited for him to get a good, long look before I crossed my arms in front of me as if I was embarrassed by him seeing me dressed like that. I explained that I ran downstairs to get a drink and used the bathroom while I was down there. He didn't say much, but his hands quickly dropped in front of his own crotch. I know what he saw had an effect on him. Promising to make sure I grab a robe from here on out, I ran up the stairs feeling his gaze on my ass that peeked out from under the bottom of the gown.

When I got into my room, I was surprised by how turned on it had made me. There's something about the combination of plotting and seeing the want in a man's eyes that makes my clit throb for release. I left my door open a crack, but I never looked in that direction. If he saw me, it would be an added bonus, but it wasn't part of my plan. Just knowing he might see me was enough.

I sat on the edge of the bed and licked my first two fingers. My back was to the door, but if I did have an audience, it would be easy to tell what I was up to. I rubbed my wet pussy and inserted a finger. It felt good, but I wished I had a toy. When I packed my things to come here, I left all of that in my room back home. I didn't think it'd be wise in case one of the kids got snoopy.

I inserted a second finger and thrusted both of them in and out, grinding against my hand. My moans were soft, and it was a struggle to keep them that way when I usually have no problem keeping quiet during solo sessions. Using my thumb, I rubbed my clit, and it sent electric waves throughout my body. The last good fucking I had was before I took this job, so my body needed this. It wouldn't be much longer.

I kept rubbing my clit and

fucking my hand. Part of me wished he would spy me and join in, but the long game would be sweeter in the end. I was right there, but I couldn't quite finish. My breathing was so shallow, and I was fucking myself hard enough to shake the bed. I had to know if he was watching me. It's what my pussy was demanding. The thrill of an onlooker was the only thing that would make me cum, but I refused to look. If he was there, it would clue him in that it was a set up for his benefit.

So instead, I drove a third finger deep into my pussy and threw my head back. A long groan escaped my lips as I was desperate to release. That's when I heard it.

There was a bump in the hall followed by quick footsteps that led to Lance's bedroom. I don't know how long he had been there, but he saw enough regardless. When my head rolled back, he must've thought he'd be seen and rushed away quickly enough to stumble. That noise sent pulsations over my clit, and my cum started flowing down my fingers.

I bit my lip to prevent myself from crying out. Wave after wave of my orgasm rocked through the walls of my wet tunnel, and I felt my juices pool up under my ass. I am a wet one. Always making a mess.

Once it was over, I sat there and waited until my breathing calmed. I would lift my heel until the pressure was on my toes and watch as my knee started to shake. The after effects of cumming were amazing. Every muscle in the body gets a work out during climax.

I changed into my regular pajamas that were child appropriate and looked at the wet spot that had spread out on the blanket. With a shrug, I climbed into bed. It could wait until morning seeing as how I stayed up late enough as it was. Besides, I'm the one who has to wash them anyway.

Chapter Two

Dear Diary,

Maybe if I wrote in this book every night, I wouldn't have so much catching up to do when I finally got around to it.

So far things are going great. My friends think I'm crazy, and they're probably right. I'm tired of hearing what did Lance do? Tori is the one who deserves it not him. They tell me I should just quit, or expose Tori for cheating. Be done with it. Where's the fun in that? Lance is spineless. He married into money, and he doesn't want to lose it. It's apparent he doesn't get to touch her accounts, but it's not like he has bills to pay aside from my nanny services. He also can't be blind to how she treats me either. If the three of us are within earshot of each other, she makes it a point to complain about me over the stupidest so called problems. I put the spoons in the drawer upside down. Are you fucking serious? That man actually talked to me about it. As far as I'm concerned, he deserves what's coming as much as she does.

Since last time, I've been working on getting closer to Lance. I can't let him become suspicious about what I'm up to. If he thinks for one moment I'm trying to seduce him, he'll put his guard up.

I have to be careful.

There are no more late night appearances in my nightie. Once is enough. From time to time, I can tell when he looks at me he's thinking about it. When he sees me at night now, it's always in comfy, family appropriate jammies, and I don't make a point of running into him every night. When I do, I ask him about his day, if he's hungry, and so on. It's more than he gets from the wife who should be doing those things.

Some days when Tori is gone and Lance is home, my cleavage may show a bit more than usual. I also make sure to squeeze in the accidental brush up against him. Whether it's allowing my hand to glide over his firm ass or making sure my boobs hit against him. Oh! There was one night when I knew he was behind me, so I turned quickly. My breasts full on pressed against his bare back. I was wearing a thin tank top, but still. That poor man ran from the room as fast as he could manage mumbling he left something in his room in the hopes of not letting me see his half-mast woody. Too late.

Meanwhile, Tori is still her worthless self. Their son had some incident in PE today. It's stupid if you ask me. How can you have the class play dodgeball then try to punish a kid for hitting someone with the ball too hard? The teacher called and wanted a parent to meet with him at the end of the school day to discuss the matter. Lance was at work, and Tori couldn't be bothered! I mistakenly thought the meeting was with the principal, and that's what I told her when she got her ass out of bed. She had me go to the meeting instead because she slept till two then woke with a hangover.

This nut job sent me in her place. As pissed as I was, at least I got out of the house away from her for a little bit. Plus, she'd actually have to watch her own kids for a while which was more than enough incentive. I really didn't think the teacher would settle for a conference with the nanny. None of my teachers would have allowed that. This was a private school, so maybe they were used to this elitist crap there. I have one, and only one, professional looking outfit. It's a black skirt suit with a pale lavender blouse. It better do the trick.

I went to the office and told them why I was there, but they had no knowledge of any dodgeball incident. Seriously? The secretary checked into it and told me I was to meet with the PE teacher, Mr. Peterson. After some instructions on how to find him, I made my way to the gym. There was a man, probably in his early forties, sitting on the bleachers wearing what looked to be the school's PE uniform. I approached him, and he gave me a puzzled look.

"Are you Mr. Peterson?" I asked.

"Yes," he said curiously, eyeing my curves.

"I'm Vicki. Vicki Sweet," I said, watching his eyes linger on my long legs. "I'm Colton's nanny."

His head snapped up and he squinted his eyes. "Tori...I mean Mrs. Rayburn sent you?"

For a fleeting moment, I thought he was upset I wasn't a parent. Then it clicked. This was no parent teacher meeting. It was an excuse to get Tori out of the house without Lance knowing what was going on. I unintentionally got the message wrong and told Tori it was the principal who called. That's why she sent me. The school office had no knowledge of anything that happened. It was a set up. This was one of her many lovers, and I foiled his plans for an afternoon bang session.

Mr. Peterson stood up and walked off the bleachers. "My apologies...Vicki? Was it?"

"Yes," I smiled. "Vicki Sweet," I said, running my tongue along my lower lip before giving it a gentle bite. The flash that went across his eyes told me he was interested.

"I'm sorry to waste your time, but it was a misunderstanding," he said, turning to walk out of the gym.

Now, it was my turn for disappointment. Granted he was

probably twice my age at least, but he was fit. He definitely looked like he would be fun to try on for size. I watched as he headed toward the boys' locker room then hurried to catch up. I reached the door just before it closed behind him. Holding it open slightly, I unbuttoned my jacket and the top couple buttons of my shirt exposing not only my cleavage, but most of my bra.

I knew he liked what he saw when he looked at me. He probably wasn't sure it was a good idea to make a move so unexpectedly. Maybe he didn't want to risk pissing Tori off. I, on the other hand, had no problems making that witch mad as hell.

Pushing the door open, there was an empty hall that led to a row of lockers blocking the rest of the room. I walked down the hall, but didn't see him. "Hello? Mr. Peterson?" I called out.

He appeared instantly from an office set off to the side. "Miss Sweet? I thought you were leaving."

I laughed softly. "Sorry again. I thought you were showing me out," I lied, walking closer to him. His eyes followed my exposed breasts as I neared him.

Mr. Peterson cleared his throat. "Miss Sweet," he began.

"Call me Vicki."

"Vicki, I can... Um, I can show you..." he fumbled finding the words. His breathing was getting shallow, and I knew he was mine.

I placed my hand on his chest and looked up at him under my long eyelashes. "Are you sure there's been a misunderstanding about this meeting?"

He inhaled sharply and tilted his head back. It was an inner struggle for him. Fucking me even once could put an end to his affair if Tori found out only he didn't know I would make sure she did. Still, it was obvious the temptation was strong.

I ran my hand down his chest over his abdomen and slid it inside the waistband of his shorts. That move made up his mind, and he grabbed my arms and pulled me close, planting a hard, deep kiss on my lips. The force of it excited me. Letting go of my arms, he yanked his shorts to his ankles, and I reached blindly to find his hard cock. I started working him with both hands while he massaged my breasts.

He put a hand on my ass and started pulling up my skirt, but it was too soon. I wiggled from his hold enough to squat down in front of him and place my mouth over his knob. Running my tongue around the head of his dick, I reached for his balls, cupping them and rolling them in my hand.

"Damn, Vicki," I heard him whisper.

I licked my other hand and started jacking him off, looking at him to see how he liked it. His head was tilted far back, and his eyes were closed. I took him in my mouth and slowly went down until I had swallowed him whole. He only let me suck him off for a minute before he backed away.

He pulled me off the floor and spun me around. "You asked for it," he sneered in my ear.

Grabbing a large section of my hair, he yanked my head back hard. God, the pulsations trembling outward from my button were intense. I wanted this man's cock now. He pushed me forward and led me to a long bench that ran near the wall under the windows. Never letting go of my hair, his other hand squeezed my breasts and pulled my bra down exposing them. Taking turns between them, he flicked and pinched the nipples. Everything he was doing was painful, but it was making me so wet.

He reached down to my knee, and lifted my leg until my foot was on the bench. Then he reached between my legs and grabbed hold of my panties, twisting them in his hand and ripped them off of me. I cried out loudly as the fabric cut into me as he pulled on them before they broke free, and he threw them on the floor.

His cock slipped into my pussy easily, and he took his time pushing his full length inside. Pulling back the same way, he moved slowly until he was completely out. I savored feeling every bit of him, but he had been so dominant until now. I needed him to fuck me. Fuck the hell out of me.

After a few times of entering me nice and slow, he said softly, "So Tori sent you to take her place?"

"Uh-huh," I answered breathlessly.

His shaft was just about to pop out of my pussy again at the end of another slow and deliberate stroke. "I hope she warned you that I'm an ass man," he stated, driving his now pussy juice lubed cock hard into my ass.

I cried out so loudly that I practically screamed. My arm flailed in front of me trying to put my hand on the window to brace myself, but I couldn't reach.

"Don't you worry your sweet ass. I've got you," he said, bringing his free arm around and holding me by my breast. His other hand tightened its grip on my hair pulling my head to the side.

He began thrusting hard and fast into my ass ripping it in two. It was the fucking I had wanted, not that sweet and innocent slow stroke crap. My moans were constant and growing louder.

"Shh," he whispered. "We can't have that." He took his hand from my breast and clamped it down hard over my mouth.

I stared out the window at the track team running laps and

wondered if they could see us were they to look in our direction. The thought of being seen made my clit start to tremble. I rubbed my clit vigorously and within seconds, my cum started flowing. My pussy was contracting violently, and the orgasm was unending. There was no way he couldn't feel it through the walls of my ass.

"Oh," he groaned. "You like having your ass murdered by my cock don't you?"

I nodded.

He chuckled. "No noise, okay?"

I nodded again.

He released my mouth and hair and shoved my back till I bent over so far, I almost fell. Then he grabbed my waist and really started plowing into me.

Dear god, the pain was severe, but so was the pleasure! I'd never experienced such an extreme combination of both. I kept one hand on my clit, and the other on the bench to steady myself. Biting my lip hard to keep quiet, I could taste blood. If there would be any drama from Tori over this, it would be worth it.

"I'm getting close," he hissed. "I'm going to cum in your mouth."

In my mouth? After he was in my ass? My eyes widened, and I wanted to shake my head no. Definitely no! But I also wanted to keep the door open for another parent teacher conference with him in the future. Fuck.

"Your mouth, okay?" he asked louder.

"Yes," I heard myself saying.

A few strokes later, and he pulled out, spinning me to face him before pushing me down on the bench. My ass cried out in pain as it landed on the hard wood surface. I was barely sitting before he rammed his cock down my throat, and I started to gag not being prepared for it.

He grabbed the back of my head to hold me still and thrust into my face. He came pretty quickly, but his load was massive. He sprayed the back of my throat for what felt like forever, and he tasted divine.

Afterward, I tossed my now ruined panties in the trash then

straightened the rest of my outfit. I found my purse where it had been dropped across the room. Digging through it, I found one of my old business cards from my short stint as a private dancer and handed it to him. "If there's any more trouble with the children, you can always call me direct," I said before leaving the locker room. I'm not sure if I'll hear from him again or not, but damn, I fucking hope I do.

When I returned to the house, Tori was already on a roll. Apparently a crock pot is a device she wasn't familiar with, so she thought dinner would be delayed even though it was almost ready. I had checked myself in the car and knew my lipstick was smeared, my hair was a mess, and my lip was split open. I left it all untouched instead of trying to clean up a bit before coming inside. Once she stopped her rant and really looked at me, she asked, "What the fuck happened to you?"

I played it dumb like I didn't know what she was talking about. Then she asked if I fell at the school while meeting with the principal.

"Oh, there was some mistake. The meeting wasn't with him," I explained, watching with glee as Tori's eyes widened. She was beginning to put two and two together to equal a butt load of great sex. Pun intended.

"It wasn't?" she asked.

"No, it was with Mr. Peterson,

but don't worry. I handled everything for you."

I heard her gasp as I walked out of the room to go upstairs and change. I'm sure she's still on the phone, yelling at the poor guy.

Chapter Three

Dear Diary,

Up until recently, I had my doubts about what I was going to do. It had nothing to do with whether I was in the right, being petty, or just a royal bitch. Anyone who knows me learns very quickly not to get on my bad side. The treatment here is unbearable.

When Lance is home, it's better. I'm not treated like an abused dog. Tori still finds opportunities to get her jabs in when he's out of the room. If he's gone? Every day it gets worse. I don't understand it. She wants him to hire a nanny, and she wants someone to take care of the house. Why intentionally and repeatedly try to make me quit?

There is something fundamentally off balance about this woman. She looks good, so there is that. I still think the only reason Lance is with her is because of her daddy's money. He doesn't want to give up the free house and life with all expenses paid.

Anyway, phase two is getting into all of her accounts. I thought it would take a while to learn all of her passcodes from unlocking her phone to her checking account login. Hold on there with your wild thoughts. I have no intentions of wire transferring money to me or anything just as foolish. To beat her, I need to know her. What is she spending the money on and where is she going? I need to be one step ahead of her.

Right after my romp at the school, I began trying to watch as secretively as possible whenever she unlocked her phone. I guess years of keeping things from Lance instilled habits in her because I couldn't see a single digit of the pin number. Then last night there was this unmistakable sound of tape. Like a roll of tape that someone was pulling extremely long pieces off. I thought the kids were getting into something. I found Tori underneath her desk with a roll of tape on the floor. As soon as she saw me, she screamed at me to get out of her office.

Office? Humph. It's a small desk in the corner of the living room, but whatever. When she left for the salon today, I checked it out. This dumb ass has a list of all of her passwords taped on the underside of her desk. You've got to be kidding me. All of her passwords are some combination of the word tease and her birthday. If they require a special character, it's the dollar sign. No surprise there. Someone should tell her if you fuck every guy you meet, you're not a damn tease.

So I've been slowly snooping through everything. Social media can be tricky. You don't want to clear notifications or show someone is online when they aren't. There's enough to start digging. It took about twenty minutes to learn that she has an order coming from Rock Solid, the huge adult entertainment company. Also, it would appear she is hooking up tonight with some guy named Todd who is in town for business. He was nothing short of gorgeous. They were to meet in the lobby bar of the Hotel Galaxy Suites. If he's passing through, it's possible he has a room there. Lucky for me, it's my day off. Unfortunately for Tori, she always runs late while I try to be early.

I swung by my parents because I had nothing sexy to wear at the Rayburn's house. Up in my old room, I dressed to the nines. I wore a sexy black dress with red stilettos. Then I showed up at the bar a good hour before she was supposed to meet him.

I had been sitting there for close to thirty minutes batting off a couple pickup lines from other men during my wait before he walked in. I recognized him immediately from his photo. He sat at the bar a little ways from me obviously not interested because he had a date. I smiled at him, and it was met with feigned interest. Talk about rude.

Taking my phone from my purse, I changed my settings to show her phone number on the caller ID for any calls or texts I might send out. It's so easy with today's technology. Like taking candy from a baby. Then I created a text to send later at the right time.

Before long, another man hit on me, and I brushed him off as well. That's when I made my move since he apparently had no desire to do so himself. I took my drink and sat down next to Todd. It made him a little nervous.

"Hi. I'm Vicki," I said, looking at him under my long lashes.

"Uh, hello. Name's Todd," he said, glancing around the room.

I smiled knowing he was probably worried Tori would walk in right then. "Everything alright?" I asked.

He took a deep breath and said, "Its fine. I'm supposed to be meeting someone at six."

"That's too bad," I told him, stirring my drink with my finger. I put my finger in my mouth slowly and sucked the alcohol off of it before looking at him again. It worked. It always works.

Todd turned his full body toward me, and asked, "What brings you here? Business?"

I shook my head and smiled devilishly. "No. I'd say pleasure."

He nodded and finished his drink. "Got a date, I see," he said, waving the bartender over.

"Not yet," I replied quickly.

The poor man suddenly coughed as he choked on my words. "What's that mean? Not yet."

I shrugged and sighed taking a

long look around the room. "It's one of my favorite places to meet men. Most are traveling through. No strings. No commitments."

His eyes widened. He was definitely intrigued. "So that's what you're after? Sex? I would think most women your age would be looking for a relationship."

I furrowed my brows at him. "I'm not ready for all that," I scoffed. "But sometimes I do have a need for a man for a little while."

The bartender came over, and he ordered a round for both of us. We sipped our drinks and talked for a few minutes. Todd kept casually stroking my arm with his fingertips, brushing the loose tendrils of my hair back, and then placed his hand on my leg. I wondered if I could convince him now before Tori "canceled" on him.

I didn't have time to decide if I wanted to go ahead and do the honors of letting him down for her. His phone dinged. I pulled mine back out, pretending it might be mine that received the notification even though I knew it was on silent.

"Well, that's no surprise," he said, reading his phone screen. "My date is running late. She's never on time."

"Lucky me," I commented, still holding my phone.

"How's that?"

I gave him a half shrug. "Well, it depends on how much time you think we have," I said with a wink.

Then I pressed send on my phone and placed it back in my purse.

Todd's phone dinged again. "Well, lucky you is right. She just cancelled," he smiled, putting his arm around my shoulder. "Shall we go upstairs?"

This is too easy. I followed him through the bar and the lobby to the elevator. As soon as the doors closed on us, he grabbed me and laid the wettest kiss on my mouth. It was unexpected and not too thrilling. Didn't matter. I was on a mission. We were fucking tonight no matter what.

The doors opened on his floor, and he led me to his room. His hands never left my body. He groped my ass and squeezed my breasts the whole way there. It was like a fumbling high schooler in a grown man's body.

Once in the room, he tore off his jacket and loosened his tie. Tossing his keys, wallet and phone on the table, he excused himself for a minute to use the bathroom. Quickly, I grabbed his phone and set it to quiet. I couldn't have the constant stream of texts and calls from Tori demanding to know where he was interrupting us. He'd probably be upset when he finally reads them all later and learns how pissed she is at him, but it's worth it to know she will soon be at the bar looking around for a guy who stood her up as far as she knows.

Then I stripped down

completely and climbed into the bed. I sat on my knees facing the bathroom door until he appeared. His mouth dropped, and the hunger lust sparkled in his eyes. "Damn girl," he growled. "I think I'm the lucky one."

He came toward me ripping off his belt and kicking off his shoes. Climbing up on the bed, he unbuttoned his shirt while I worked on his pants. Taking his near flaccid cock in my hands I was a little offended that the sight of my nude body didn't have some effect on him, but it didn't take long for him to perk up and stand at attention.

His shirt was off by now, and I was almost pushed out of the way when he took over yanking off his slacks. He was eager and in a hurry. There wouldn't be much in the way of foreplay judging by this.

All that was left was his socks when he pushed me back on the bed and began teasing my tits with his teeth. I let him play for a minute before forcing him onto his back. I bent my head over his hard cock and playfully licked his knob. I heard him suck in his breath. Slowly, I took the tip in my mouth then deliberately eased my mouth over his full shaft as slowly as I could manage. Once I had him in my throat, he began bucking against me wildly. Amateur. He had a lot to learn.

I lifted my mouth off of him and

scooted back until I could straddle his face pressing my pussy down on his mouth. He needed no encouragement. Todd was all over the place with it. Licking my pussy, darting his tongue in and out, teasing my clit, fingering me, and even gently teasing the rim of my asshole as if he wasn't sure I'd allow it. Every time I got him in my mouth, he started bucking like a wild bull. It amused me because after Mr. Peterson, I thought Tori had great taste in lovers. There was no time, rather no need, to train him tonight. With his lack of skill, I thought the only way my needs were going to be taken care of would be if I was on top.

Lifting off of his face, I straddled

his cock and gently lowered myself, guiding him inside me with my hand. He started thrusting into me hard, so I turned my head back and whispered, "Let me."

He took that one simple instruction well. I started grinding into him slowly at first then building momentum. Whenever it started to get hot, he'd spring into action forcing me to tame him back down again. I found the position I needed. Right there on top of him with a slight tilt to my body, he hit the G-Spot perfectly. My pussy convulsed and contracted around him, and he felt it. He grabbed my hips and held me hard against him while he fucked me.

I had been wrong. There was

only one way this was going to work, but this wasn't it. I rolled off of him and laid down on the bed letting him get on top. I hooked my angles on his shoulders, so he could fold me in half tilting my pussy up. Todd thrusted into me fast and furious like it was a race, and he had to come in first. Pun intended.

That sweet mix of pleasure and pain from this position sent my pussy into overdrive. I started coming hard and continuously as every stroke hit the sweet spot. My tight walls spasmed around his cock and sent torrents of cum raining down over him. I could feel my juices dripping out down my ass and found myself hoping he might accidentally slip into the wrong hole. My intense orgasms urged him on. His stamina was impressive. Tears were streaming down my cheeks and the room was spinning around me before he grunted and collapsed on top of me spewing deep inside.

It took a while to catch my breath, but once I did, I began the search for my clothes to get dressed. "Leaving so soon?" he asked.

I smiled at him and climbed back in the bed and gave him a quick kiss. "I have to get going."

"Can I see you again?"

"Yes," I lied, knowing it would never happen.

"Give me your number. I'll get

ahold of you when I'm in town."

I grabbed my phone off the dresser and told him to give me his digits, so I can send a text. That way he could add my number later. He recited the number for me then I asked if I could take a picture to put with his contact on my phone. I laid down next to him, still naked, and took a head and shoulders picture of us side by side in bed. Not only did I add it to his contact in my phone, but with her giddy, partner in crime consent, I added it to my best friend's contact as well changing her name to Todd.

As soon as I arrived back at the Rayburn's household, I made sure to leave my phone lying face up at all times. It would only be a matter of time before Tori saw a text from my friend Jodi appear on the screen with Todd's name and picture. It hasn't happened yet, but it will.

Chapter Four

Dear Diary,

The next day, Tori's package was delivered. I recognized the label. Rock Solid goes out of their way to make their shipments look discreet, but it's easy to spot when you know how it looks. When it came, Tori was in the shower, barely awake and getting ready for her day in the middle of the afternoon. It was almost time for me to pick up the kids from the school, so I left a little bit early, taking the box with me.

Parking on the side of a gas station near the school, I opened it up to see what new goodies I had courtesy of Tori. They was quite the assortment of cock rings, lubes, and butt plugs. A powerhouse stim really caught my eye. It looked like one I had been thinking about getting, but was too expensive. Thank you, Tori. There was also a full sized bottle of banana flavored lube. I opened it and took a taste. That shit was delicious. It was definitely something to try out. I put everything in my tote bag, and tossed the packaging in the dumpster before going to the school.

As soon as I walked in the door of the Rayburn's house, Tori was all over me asking if a package had been delivered. I played it off like I didn't know anything about it even suggesting maybe she should check with the neighbors in case it was delivered wrong. Fat chance of her owning up to it being hers if they did receive it even though her name had been clearly labeled on the front.

That began my entry into phase three a little earlier than I had planned. I needed to piss her off completely. More so, I needed to set her up to look like an unreasonable crack pot who jumped my case for no other reason than she thought she was better than me. The timing couldn't be more perfect because the next day she saw Todd's face appear on my phone screen.

The three of us were in the

kitchen having a little pow-wow because Tori's folks were coming for dinner in a week or two. Lance was going to cook out that night. I would be needed to chase the kids through the yard and watch them in the pool, so the adults could have time to themselves. Not a problem.

While they were discussing details, my phone rang, and I saw Todd's face knowing it was probably my friend instead. I very politely asked Tori if she could hand me my phone as she was right next to it. The look she had when she saw Todd's picture with me right next to him! He had already stood her up basically, and by now, she probably learned about the woman he met at the bar. Seeing the realization that it was me? Priceless.

Tori immediately started yelling and telling me to leave. I was no longer welcome there. Lance stepped in and tried to calm her down, but she had flipped her shit. I kept asking what had I done and acted like I was upset while she kept carrying on. Finally, her husband asked her what I did, and she said I knew exactly what happened. Again, I acted confused and innocent which caused Tori to laugh hysterically claiming she knew what I was up to, and it wasn't going to work.

Long story short, I made her look psychotic. She couldn't come out with it in front of her husband and admit what she was pissed about. It just kept building from there. I took advantage of every opportunity to make her look like a crazy person. Whenever I knew Lance was nearby, I'd accidentally drop or spill something. Tori would start screaming at me for it, and her husband came to my defense. When she wasn't around, I made sure he knew that was how she had acted since my first day here.

It was only a matter of time until she tried to get revenge. All of the toys I stole from her were painstakingly hidden. Some I kept in my car just to make sure they were safe, but I did need a couple around for when the mood strikes.

I took the stim that had been in her package and left it under my pillow. It would be an easy and quick discovery. A smarter person might have realized it was deliberate. Luckily, I knew intelligence was one trait this woman lacked.

Sure enough, just minutes after leaving it there, I was in the kitchen preparing dinner when she walked in, waving it around and cussing me up one side then down the other. I was nothing but a low life thief, and my days were numbered. Trying to tell her it was mine, and I was sorry I left it out only made her anger increase because she knew it was hers. It was from the box that had been stolen off the porch, and she detailed the embarrassing calls to customer service of both the Rock Solid business and the shipping service to get the order replaced. I maintained my innocence throughout.

In the end, she tore apart my room looking for the rest of her items. None of them were there. I made sure of it. Nothing was untouched. Even my mattresses were flipped off the bed. She let me know I needed to clean up the mess before she left for the evening.

When Lance came home, he found me crying in the kitchen. I plucked my eyebrows to get the waterworks started then immersed myself with sad memories to keep them flowing until he got there. Of course he asked what was wrong, but I refused to tell him. He went upstairs and called for me. The mess was left almost completely untouched, and I happened to forget to close my bedroom door. Silly me.

He insisted on an explanation, and I told him the truth. My version of it anyway. I confessed his wife had a package of sex toys that were delivered to the wrong address or stolen off the porch. She found one of mine in my room that must be similar to what she ordered, so she tore apart my bedroom looking for the rest. It was easy to convince him as he'd already spied me taking my business in my own hands. He could easily believe I had toys here.

Apologizing to me the whole time, he helped me set my room back to right. Some of it I had taken care of before he got home. The only clothing left strewn about were my sexiest panties. I was in complete control of what he saw and what thoughts were planted in his mind. He even snooped through her dresser to bring me the toy she had confiscated. It was only a matter of time now before I brought my plan to a head.

When she got home, he was waiting for her. I was woken up to the fight from the next room. He defended me the entire time. The best part of what I overheard was when he demanded to know why she never felt well enough to fuck her husband, but had the need for sex toys to take care of herself. Yes, everything was moving along just fine.

The next night he was off duty, and she seduced him. It was sickening. Even poor Lance wasn't really sure how to respond. They headed upstairs at the same time I put the children to bed. In my room, I could hear them, but I needed more than that. I stripped down and put on my robe, grabbed the toy that had caused all the problems the day before, and creeped into the hallway.

Their bedroom door wasn't quite closed all the way, and I wondered if it had been left like that on purpose. It was just not quite closed enough to latch, so I pushed on it gently. The sound of Tori's moans immediately grew louder once there was a small crack in the doorway. As much as I hated the woman, the sound of her being pleasured hit the sweet spot between my legs, and I felt the throbbing begin.

I slowly pushed on the door a little more and spied them through the small crack along the frame. It was a perfect angle to the bed. Tori was riding him slow and hard. Her head was tilted back and her eyes were closed probably imagining one of her many affairs was beneath her instead. Lance was caressing her breasts with both hands.

I pushed the button at the

bottom of the stim to turn it on and paused to see if the hum was noticed. Neither of them flinched. I spread out the opening of my robes and ran it along my inner thighs and lips before bringing it to my clit. A soft moan escaped me before I clamped my mouth closed to prevent any more from slipping out. I hoped Lance would look my way, but I couldn't risk being seen by Tori.

The outline of Lance's cut chest was like a masterpiece, and I followed it down as far as I could before Tori's leg blocked the view. I longed to see his shaft. I wanted to embed the image of it in my mind, and I had hoped they might change positions before they were through.

Tori was grinding into him, building herself toward climax slowly. I slipped two fingers into my dripping pussy and thrust them inside me to her rhythm. For a bitch, her body was sexy as hell.

I was so preoccupied with staring at her that I don't know how long Lance had been watching me before I noticed. Without turning my head, I saw him out of the corner of my eyes. He dropped his hands to his wife's hips, but his full attention was on the doorway. Perfect.

Untying the belt with my free hand, I let the robe fall open, partially exposing my naked body to him. I saw the flash in his eye and knew he appreciated the view.

I kept working my pussy hard, but I cupped one breast and lifted it up. Tilting my chin down, I brought my tongue to my tit and started to tease it. Lance's mouth fell open as he watched, and I saw the intense desire in his eyes increase. There was no doubt he wanted nothing more than for me to join them in that moment, and I wouldn't have minded the company myself even though we both knew I couldn't.

Soon I forgot all about stealing glances at him although I don't doubt he never took his eyes off me. In fact, I even stopped worrying that Tori might actually look at the man she was fucking instead of keeping her thoughts on the one she was fantasizing about and catch a glimpse of me in the doorway in the process. All I concerned myself with was my next orgasm, and it was coming fast.

This little stim was driving my clit mad with pleasure. I slid a third finger inside and thrust into my pussy hard, ramming my hand against me. Practice allowed me to expertly hold the stim in place while I fucked my fingers. I pinched and teased my tits with my other hand. I had my own rhythm now, not needing to follow Tori's speed any longer. I pressed my shoulder blades into the door jam, and arched my lower back. It was close. I thrust against my hand hard wishing it was Lance's cock inside me.

Closing my eyes, I pictured him in front of me. His muscular chest pressed hard against my breasts as he lifted me, and I wrapped my legs around his waist. His hard cock entered my pussy in my fantasy, and that was all the push I needed to hit my orgasm. My whole body convulsed and fell forward as wave after wave rocked me, and pussy juice flowed over my hand.

I heard him grunting and realized I was making him cum as well. He had been watching me that whole time. Seeing me cum pushed him over the edge. I hurried down the hall to my room before Tori had a chance to catch me. On my way, I heard her scold him for not giving her warning because she hates cleaning up after he cums inside her. It made me smile because I'm fairly certain Lance knows the woman down the hall wouldn't have minded having his load shot deep inside her pussy or down her throat, whichever he preferred.

Chapter Five

Dear Diary,

Two entries back to back. It's a record for me.

It's my day off, but Lance had to work. His schedule has been crazy due to the force being understaffed. I saw him close to noon when he made his way downstairs. I was in running shorts and a tank top, relaxing in the kitchen.

As soon as he saw me, a look flashed on his face that told me he was remembering my show last night as his wife fucked him. Because I made sure not to directly glance his way, he couldn't be certain if I knew he had seen me or not.

"Good morning," he said, upbeat and cheerful from finally getting his blue balls drained.

"Morning," I said quietly.

"Everything all right?"

"Yeah," I forced a yawn. "Late night. Didn't get much sleep."

His eyes widened and his hands moved to cover his crotch. I'm not sure if it was instinctive since he knew what I was referring to, or if it was because he didn't want me to see the rock hard bulge that was forming.

"Oh," he finally mumbled.

I smiled at him and stood up. "Getting ready to take a nap now. Need my energy for later."

"Big plans?" he laughed.

I smiled coyly. "I have a date," I said, before walking out of the room. Always leave them feeling like they have competition.

There was no date, but I needed a good fucking. After Todd's amateur rodeo and watching Tori get all the dick, my pussy was crying out for attention. It left me on the verge of getting ahold of the PE teacher from the school. If it wasn't the weekend, I might have just dropped by unannounced. I decided to head out to the same bar where I met up with Todd to see what hit on me. I had hope of catching another traveling salesman so to speak.

After a short nap and a long

shower, I got ready to go out. I wore my tightest red dress. It was sleeveless and hugged all the right places. Once I was ready, I quietly snuck out the backdoor off the kitchen even though I park on the street. I didn't want to suffer the third degree from Tori who would probably assume I was out sucking the dick of someone else she had in her pocket.

It didn't take long for the guys to start swarming after I arrived at the bar. If any of them asked the bartender about me, they might be told I had picked up guys there before. Greg really caught my attention. He was dressed in jeans and a T-Shirt and was covered in tattoos. Not my normal type, but there was something about the way he talked that made me want to see them all. The flirtation started to rise and get heated, and I knew I was about to get my desires quenched.

Greg leaned over and whispered in my ear, "I want to fuck you until you beg me to stop."

I smiled at him and said, "That sounds like a fun night."

He shook his head and slapped the bar hard. "I'm about to throw your ass up here and eat you out in front of God and everybody."

"What's stopping you?" I accepted his challenge.

He shook his head and half moaned, half laughed. "Before I take you out of here to somewhere with a little more privacy, you wouldn't happen to have a friend for my buddy over there, would you?"

I looked in the direction where he nodded and saw his friend sitting in a booth alone. I had noticed the man before. He couldn't stop staring at me the entire evening, but I had no idea the two of them were together. His friend wasn't as good looking as Greg, but his chest was massive. He was physically fit, but quite large. I was intrigued.

"Sorry, sweetie, I don't," I said.

Greg looked at the counter and nodded. Probably trying to decide how to break the news to his friend that he was leaving him solo.

"But that's alright. There's plenty of me to go around," I offered.

Greg snapped his head back to me so fast I could feel a draft. I just smiled mischievously at him.

He turned to me, and said, "Damn! I am glad I met you."

I laughed. "Where are we going?"

"My place."

"Let me use the ladies room, and I'll be ready to go."

The guys hung around in the lobby for me probably thinking I was full of shit and about to bolt. When I appeared, they looked quite happy to see me. Greg introduced his friend as Scott. I walked outside with them and climbed up into his pickup truck, sitting in the middle between them. Both of them put a hand on my leg, but by the time we stopped, it was so much more. Greg was already teasing my pussy under my dress, and Scott had my tits exposed. They couldn't wait to get the party started.

Greg's place turned out to be a mechanic's garage that had a room in the back with a bed. While I wondered how often it was used for nights like this, it looked relatively picked up, and the smell of the dryer sheets was distinct. At least the bedding was clean.

I sat on the edge of the bed, bending my knee to place my foot on the bed. Greg was on the bed next to me in a flash, yanking my panties down my legs. Meanwhile, Scott dropped his jeans to his ankles revealing a rather large cock that was stiff and ready with pre-cum glistening on the tip. He stood in front of me, and I ran my tongue around the full girth in a swirl all the way to the base to lube him up before closing my mouth over the tip. I sucked hard and fast on the head of his dick, and his arms flailed out for support. There was nothing nearby to brace himself on. Then I went down slowly, taking him in my mouth until I could feel him in the back of my throat.

Greg was working my pussy with one hand and fighting his pants with the other. When he realized his friend was already getting some action, he told me to get on all fours. Letting Scott's cock slide from my mouth, I did as I was told. Greg quickly mounted me from behind, slipping his cock into my pussy.

There's no denying I've been needing this. The best stress relief in the world is a good pounding, and Tori is a bottomless pit of stress causing antics. Greg slid his full length inside of me a few times before picking up a faster rhythm. I was already to my first climax before Scott kneeled on the bed in front of my face.

Taking his cock back in my mouth, I began to bob my head on his shaft matching the pace Greg was using to fuck my pussy.

Moaning all around his impressive cock as Greg repeatedly brought me to orgasm easily. Each thrust of his cock increased my enthusiasm and hunger for Scott's shaft. I couldn't get enough of these two. I sucked that cock down my throat like it was the most delicious meal I'd ever had.

Soon, Scott had other plans. He told his buddy it was time to switch up. Greg moaned, and I got the feeling he didn't want to move from where he was, but Scott convinced him by raving about how great my mouth felt. They swapped positions in no time. I was already in full swing devouring my taste off of Greg's cock while Scott teased me with his tip.

"Ready for this, Vicki?" he asked.

"Mmm-hmm," I moaned, not letting Greg's stiff member slip from my lips.

Scott chuckled, "We'll see about that."

He leaned forward and thrust his large cock inside me slowly, and it felt like I was being split in two. He pulled out completely then thrust inside me hard. My whole body lunged forward from the force, but he grabbed my hips to steady me. His cock tore into me sending wave after wave of shuddering orgasms through my pussy, massaging his dick in the process.

I moaned non-stop on Greg's cock and was so distracted by how

Scott was destroying my snatch, I didn't read the signs that Greg was close to release. The hot liquid that sprayed the back of my throat surprised me at first, but I gulped down every drop of it before licking his shaft clean.

"Bout time there, bud," Scott said when Greg backed away from me pulling up his pants.

In a blur, I was pushed forward and to the side. Scott laid on his back on the bed. "All yours, little lady," he said, clasping his hands behind his head.

My box was already sore, and it stung as I straddled him and began to ease down on his cock.

"Don't disappoint, now. Fuck me like you mean it."

His words sent tremors through me, and I started to cum before I had his full length inside me.

"That's it. Show me how much you love this cock."

I eased down until he was completely inside, moaning out loudly as my body caved and made room for him. "I do love your cock, Scott." I started grinding into him slowly, and my body shook involuntarily from the near constant climax I was experiencing.

"I don't think you do," he teased. "Convince me."

Grinding into him harder and faster, my moans continued to grow louder. I threw my head back and closed my eyes enjoying how full he made me feel. My pussy gripped his cock and sent cum soaking down him in torrents.

"That's better," Scott said, "but I'm still not convinced."

I whipped my head back down to look him in the eye and leaned forward into him. Hooking my ankles around his legs, I started riding him as fast as I could. My mouth fell open, and one long, shrill moan escaped my lips and didn't stop until he came.

Scott's cock engorged with cum, and I thought he'd burst right through my walls. The strain was that intense. He pumped what felt like a gallon of his cum deep inside me, and my eyes rolled back from sheer pleasure. My leg twitched involuntarily from the strain of the repeated orgasms I'd had and seemed to keep time with his release. Damn, it was an amazing fuck.

Chapter Six

Dear Diary,

Things have been pretty much typical around here the last few days. After my last night off, I needed some time to recover. I've been hanging out in the evenings trying to lay low as much as possible hoping Tori wouldn't work me like a dog. Just acting like a fly on the wall observing everything that's going on.

Tori has decided to add church activities to her long list of bullshit excuses to get out of the house. Supposedly now, she belongs to a bible study group and has decided to attend a weekly women of the church meeting. Funny... She seems awfully involved in her church for someone who never attends services.

I only have three things to say about it. One, it's obviously a lie. It's the same as her other so called activities to get her out of the house. She's stupid enough to think her husband doesn't suspect a thing, but he has to know something is up. Two, isn't this the type of thing that would send you straight to hell? If you lie and say you're going to a bible study group just to get out of the house to cheat on your husband with whoever your new flavor of the week is, wouldn't that warrant an immediate first class ticket straight to hell?

Lastly, I'm curious as to why she chose church as a cover. It makes me wonder if she's not fucking a preacher. If she is, I have to say I'm impressed.

I started making sure I deliberately smile and laugh whenever he's around. If they're both present, I act like I'm scared of her. I'd already been doing this, but it was more low-key. I've stepped it up a few notches. Whenever he's gone, and she tries to crack the whip, I'm quick to point out what he has to say about my job duties. I had to find some way to get under her skin as the fake calls from the boy toy I stole from her don't seem to have an effect anymore.

Also, I found the perfect nightie for my situation when I was cleaning up the mess she made tearing apart my room not long ago. I hardly ever wear it, so I had forgotten about it. It's very appropriate and covers everything, but if I stand just right in the light, you could see every inch of my body through it. I tried it out immediately, making sure Lance could see the skimpy thong I was wearing. By the tightened expression on his face, I could tell he not only saw it, but it had the desired results I wanted as well.

Everything must be working as I planned. I overheard them argue last night. She's not at all happy with me and wants me gone. Tori even made the claim that she's convinced I'm trying to sleep with her husband. Of course, Lance thought she was over-reacting. Thank you, Tori. If he didn't have the thought in his head before, he certainly does now. You have no idea how much of a shove you just gave him in the right direction. People hate being accused. If you make an accusation like that to an innocent person, they'll act on it and make it the truth. Lance reminded her that all the other nannies before me barely lasted a week, and at least I stuck around. So that was the end of it.

It's my night off, but Lance is at work. I didn't really have any plans and was going to hang out here in my room until Tori insisted I help out tonight because she had a meeting, so she wanted me to watch the children. I told her I couldn't because I had a date. She probably would've argued I could reschedule, but I quickly disappeared to my room to get ready.

Not wanting to make a liar out of myself, I went on to the Meet Now dating app to find someone to spend some time with tonight. Hunter looked hot from his profile pictures, so I face timed him to make sure he looked just as good in person. Once I was certain I wasn't being catfished, I laid it all out for him. I said I'm only looking for a bit of fun. It's your choice. We could go to a bar where you will shell out a lot of money to get us both drunk only to have horrible sex in the backseat of a car that neither of us will barely remember tomorrow, or we could skip the pretenses and go straight to a motel. You get the room, and I'll bring a twelve pack. We can skip right to the good part for as long as we'd like. That poor man acted like he had just won the lottery.

I met up with him at the room. We each grabbed a beer and talked for a few minutes trying to become at ease around one another. I meant it when I said I was only looking for action. Things were moving too slow for me. I reached behind my back and unzipped my dress then slowly let it slip down over my body to the floor around my ankles. I wasn't wearing panties. You never know when you may find yourself in need of easy access. I let him admire my garter and bra for several moments.

"You weren't kidding, were you?" he asked.

"I never joke about sex," I said, reaching around again to unfasten my bra.

"No," Hunter said quickly. "Leave it."

I smiled at him and lifted one leg to put my foot on the edge of the bed. "What about my heels?" I asked.

Hunter groaned, and a devilish

look passed over his face. "Yeah, leave them on too."

He scrambled to start ripping his clothes off and came up behind me half naked. Pulling my head back hard by my hair with one hand, he reached down with the other to stroke my already wet pussy.

This is what I want. Just sex. No strings. No awkward goodbyes. No promises of phone calls or future dates that no one intends to keep. All I want, what I need, is a good old fashioned fucking with a stranger. People act like there's something wrong with it, but sometimes, it's better than what you get from a relationship.

Hunter started to bend me over

by pushing forward with the hold he had on my hair, and he moved his hand around my hips to begin fingering me from behind. After the last fucking I had, I was still a little sore in some places, so I wanted a more relaxed position this time. I wiggled my way out from in front of him, and he let go of my hair allowing me to move.

I climbed up on the bed and laid back lifting both legs next to each other straight in the air. Before I slowly began separating them to the side, I could already hear Hunter scurrying out of the rest of his clothes. Once my legs were fully spread to the side, he made a lunge onto the bed and buried his face straight into my box.

He furiously went after my pussy with everything he had. I rested my ankles on his shoulders and grinded into his face forcefully. I wanted it all. There would be no holding back from me. He grabbed my hips and dug in with his fingertips trying not to give me much room to move, but it wasn't enough to stop me. After several orgasms, I reached down to pull him up.

Hunter grunted and shook his head telling me in his own way he wasn't full yet. I bent my knees a little more and pulled one foot back then dug my heel into his shoulder.

"Ow," he cried, pulling back quickly while looking at me like he was pissed.

I did the same with my other foot as well, but not as hard. "Do what I say, and it won't hurt," I told him.

His eyes sparkled, "Yes, ma'am. Where do you want me?"

I leaned up on my elbows with my feet still on his shoulders. "Fuck me like you own it," I told him sternly.

In one quick move, he lifted his arms, throwing both of my feet off his shoulders. He leaned it with perfect aim, and drove the length of his cock inside my pussy as he brought his weight down on top of me. The angle of my box with my body bent in half like that brought my g-spot into the perfect position for Hunter to hit it with every stroke.

"Ahhhhhh!" I screamed out from the surprise of being filled so quickly. Hunter thrust into me with a steady rhythm that easily brought several orgasms out of me. His cock felt amazing each time he thrust it inside, and when he pulled back, I squeezed the tight walls of my pussy around him trying to prevent his cock from moving.

"I'm getting close," he said in my ear.

I smiled knowing I would soon be filled with his cum, but he had other plans.

"I want to cum in your mouth," he said.

I nodded and then said, "Yes, I'd like that."

A few strokes later, Hunter pulled out and hopped up next to me on the bed. I rolled to the side and grabbed his shaft with my mouth. After a couple quick licks, I pushed my head down, swallowing him whole.

Hunter wasn't expecting it, and his arms swung out to grab my shoulders. Once he steadied his balance, his head rolled back and a long guttural moan escaped his lips. I sucked him hard with his full length in my mouth, and he started to cum. It felt amazing having that hot liquid coat my throat.

When he was finished, I laid back on the bed and rested for a few minutes. I loved how sore my pussy felt after a great fucking. I like the throbbing that pounds like a drum throughout my box reminding me of how well it'd been tended to. I lay there enjoying the after bliss almost forgetting Hunter was still in the room. That is until he spoke and ruined it.

"What do you say we order a pizza and find a movie to watch?" He laid down next to me and propped himself up on one arm leaning down near my face. "We could always go for round two later if you'd like."

Ugh. Why'd he have to make it sound like a real date? I told it to him straight from the get go. All I was after was a hook up. Nothing more, nothing less. I wouldn't have minded another go with his delectable body if he had kept it to pure, unadulterated physical needs only.

"Sorry. I have early commitments. I can't stay out long," I said, rising off the bed before I was finished speaking. It didn't take long to get dressed since the only item I took off was my dress. I threw it over my head and grabbed my purse on my way to the door.

"Well, can I see you again sometime?" Hunter asked.

Not if I can help it. "Sure. Just text me," I answered, without looking back and closing the door behind me. I knew he didn't have my number, and I had his profile blocked on the Meet Now app

before I got back to the Rayburn's
house.

Chapter Seven

Dear Diary,

My time here is almost up. I'm not so much worried about Tori finally getting her way and firing me as I am that I will soon lose my temper and go off on the bitch. I have to get the rest of my plan wrapped up fast.

Yesterday, I began my next phase which is solely about dropping little hints around the both of them. The idea is to let Tori know I am fully aware of the slut that she is, and to help Lance reaffirm any suspicions he already has. I mean he has to know his wife is fucking half the town, but if I can clue him in onto some strange that he doesn't know about, I'll be content.

They were in the living room, and I was loading the dishwasher when I had a great idea of how to begin this phase. Tori had worn a hot dress out the other night, but spilled cocktail sauce on it. It was at the cleaners. From the kitchen, I called out that I'd get ready soon to pick up the kids to have enough time to get her blue dress.

Just as I hoped, they were discussing why her blue dress was at the dry cleaner before I even made my way upstairs. Tori is the world's worst liar when put on the spot. She needs time to prepare her story. The quickest defense she had was to say she didn't know what I was talking about which meant when I reappeared, she confronted me about it in front of her husband. The stupid woman actually tried to wink at me secretly and give me looks suggesting I play along. I pretended not to see them.

"You must be confused. You picked up the dry cleaning last week," she said, with a glare encouraging me to agree.

"Yes, but this is the dress I dropped off for you on Wednesday."

"What dress?" Lance asked.

I smiled sweetly at him. "The light blue dress."

Tori looked like she could spit nails.

I continued, "You know, the one with the low cut bodice. It had something red on it. Cocktail sauce, right?" I asked her.

Tori laughed nervously. "Oh, that's right. I forgot. The girls and I grabbed a bite when we were out the other night, and I clumsily dropped a shrimp."

Looking confused, I said, "No, it was the bible study group."

Tori would've murdered me then if it weren't for her husband being a witness. "You are mistaken. It was my girls' night."

Headed toward the door, I said, "Well, I hope they were able to save it then since that means you waited three days for me to drop it off."

I left for the school knowing at

the very least, I put something in Lance's mind to think about. He would be at work by the time I got back, but luckily, the kids had soccer practice. I wouldn't have to come straight back to the house to face Tori's wrath. With any luck, she'd be too busy preparing for whatever fling she had lined up tonight to give me a second thought. It was better than I hoped. She was gone when we got back to yet another supposed meeting at the church.

I went about the night helping them with their homework and fixing dinner. Once they were bathed and in bed, I settled in the living room to watch some television since it was a bigger screen than the one in my room. I dozed off and woke to headlights pulling in the drive. Not good. If it was Tori, she'd have a field day about me using the family room for personal reasons. God, I can't stand that woman.

Quickly, I ran to the kitchen and started unloading the dishwasher. I didn't need her to have an actual reason to be mad at me right now as stupid as the reason might be. She had made it clear on more than one occasion I was not to be in the family room unless supervising the children. In my rush, I didn't even notice the time. If I had, I would've known it was Lance who was going to be walking through the door not his wife.

As soon as I saw him, I smiled big time. It wasn't part of the whole be sugary sweet to him routine. It was relief. "How was your day?" I asked.

He glanced around suspiciously before answering. Not sure what that was about. I asked if he was hungry then offered to heat up dinner for him. He insisted he was more than capable, but I told him it was no trouble. He went upstairs to change while I got it ready for him. After he ate, I took care of his dishes.

When he asked about his wife, his attitude changed. She still wasn't home, and it was after midnight. Who knew a meeting of church ladies would run so late? Lance was livid. "I work my ass off. I put my life on the line every time I leave this house. Yet, the only person who gives a fuck about me is the damn nanny!'

He looked at me, and his face softened. "I'm sorry. I didn't mean anything by that."

I shook my head. "It's fine. I understand. Don't worry about it."

Lance paced back and forth. "I mean how hard would it be to get a warm greeting from time to time? Maybe a massage after a long shift? Is that so much to ask."

"And a blow job," I agreed, folding my arms across my chest.

He stopped in his tracks and looked at me. His eyes blinked

repeatedly.

I threw my hand to my mouth pretending I didn't mean to say it out loud, and said, "Oh, it slipped out. I'm just saying. I'd give my husband a massage and a blow job to help him relax. He would deserve it, you know?" I shrugged.

Lance continued to stare at me, and it was easy to see what was going through his mind. He wanted to take me right then. Mostly because he had needs his wife was ignoring, and I was available. There may have been a little serves her right about Tori going through his head too. It wasn't time yet, so I tried to act a little uncomfortable and excuse myself for bed.

I smiled when he paused as he

passed my room later. If he had knocked, I would've given him the fucking of his life, but he didn't. That's all right, Lance. All in good time.

Then today, I couldn't believe my luck when Tori not only sent a text claiming she was at a friend's and too drunk to drive home, but wanted me to be the one to break the news to Lance after his shift. It was too perfect. When he came home, I did a wash, rinse, repeat of the night before making sure he had something to eat. He didn't even bother asking about his wife this time.

Once he was settled in the recliner in the living room to relax, I slipped off my robe revealing the sexy nightie he had already seen me in and walked up behind him. I gently placed my hands on his shoulders and began rubbing them.

He jumped in his chair and looked behind him. When he first saw me, he opened his mouth to object, but then his eyes trailed downward to what I was wearing. It shut him up real quick.

I began rubbing his shoulders again, and he turned back in his chair. "You know I didn't mean you had to do this when I mentioned it last night," he said quietly.

"It's alright. I don't mind. Besides, I've been told I'm good at it."

He closed his eyes and rested

his head back. "That you are."

I worked his shoulders good for several minutes until I was certain most of the stress he was feeling had slipped away. I stopped and walked to the front of the chair. He didn't move except to follow me with his eyes. I stood in front of him and smiled seductively before dropping to my knees. He leaned forward then.

"What are you doing?" he asked, not sounding as frantic as I expected him to.

"Exactly what I said I'd do if you were mine," I replied, running my hand along the waistband of the sweats he was wearing. "Giving you the welcome home treatment you deserve."

I slid my hand inside the waistband, but he caught my wrist and stopped me. He looked into my eyes and didn't say a word. Licking my lips, I tried to free my hand from his, but he wouldn't loosen his grip.

"We can't," he said, looking around.

"It's okay. Tori messaged that she won't be home tonight."

Lance didn't say anything, but I saw the expression on his face change. He was hurt. He was hurt by how his wife ran around on him so often and without a care. He was hurt because it was easy to see I knew what his wife was really up to when she spewed her outrageous lies about where she'd been. For a moment, I wasn't sure what he'd do, but then he let go of my wrist and settled back into his chair. It was all the green light I needed.

I released his cock from his sweats, and he was already hard. Lance had a perfectly defined shaft. It was thick, long, and he kept everything very well maintained. I relish that in a man. I looked at it for several moments without realizing what I was doing, just admiring how perfect it looked and imagining it would taste and feel the same.

He interrupted my thoughts. "So are you just gonna stare at it all night?"

It snapped me back to what I should be doing, and I looked up at him with a smirk. Not taking my eyes off him, I licked my hand then wrapped it around his member and started pumping up and down on him. I placed my mouth over his knob and gave it a good, hard suck until he groaned. Bobbing my head up and down, I swirled my tongue all around his cock until his breathing became fast and moans started escaping his lips easily.

"Mmm," I moaned. "You like that?" I asked, removing my mouth only for a second.

His reply was to grab the back of my head and push my head down while he thrusted into my throat. I took that as a yes. He was too long for me to deep throat for a lengthy period of time, so I eased up and wrapped my hand around the base. I stroked him while sucking and licking from the top. I kept a smooth constant rhythm in everything I did, knowing he would cum soon.

"Damn, Vicki," he cried out as he shot his load in my mouth.

I licked my lips and looked up under my eyelids at him. As I stood up, I leaned far into him, exposing my breasts perfectly through the neckline of the nightie I wore. With my mouth nearly touching his ear, I whispered, "Anytime, Lance."

After that, I left the room and headed to bed. I knew he would have regrets, but I also knew it would be better for him to work through them quickly. That wouldn't be easy to do if the woman

who just helped him cheat was still
lingering around.

Chapter Eight

Dear Diary,

Last night was amazing. I wondered how he'd act today. Would he regret it? Would his guilt cause him to fire me? I had certainly hoped not. I wanted the chance to really rock his world before that happened. I needn't have worried. It was as though nothing took place between us.

Tori was gone again tonight, but for a valid reason this time. There was an anniversary dinner at her parents' house. Lance was supposed to attend with her, but he pretended to have some type of stomach virus to get out of it. It was no sweat off her back. She was probably thankful he wasn't coming.

I got the kids tucked into bed then went back downstairs. Lance was in the kitchen, and the way he looked at me... It was easy to see he wanted round two. He started to make his way toward the living room, but I grabbed his hand instead to pull him back. He stopped and looked at me, so I nodded toward the stairs.

Dropping his hand, I walked slowly up the back stairs knowing he was fast at my heels. I made sure to stick my ass out a little more than usual to flaunt it right in his face. It caught me off guard when he leaned in and gently bit it, and I giggled. It was like taking candy from a baby.

I led him into my room, and he closed the door behind him. Standing next to my bed, I lifted my sundress off over my head and tossed it aside. I wasn't wearing anything underneath.

Lance sucked his breath in through his teeth at the sight of my naked body. I don't mean to brag, but I know I have a body that will drive any man mad with desire. If there had been hesitation at all in him, it disappeared as soon as he caught sight of me.

Taking a step toward him, I put my hands on his chest and ran them down to the bottom hem of his shirt. I started to lift it off him when he grabbed my hands and moved them off. For a moment, I thought this was it. He was going to end it before we began.

Instead, he turned me around and pushed me back on the bed. I sat there with my legs dangling off the edge and propped up on both elbows. "I want to watch," he said.

I raised an eyebrow at him. I knew what he was talking about, but I was hoping we were in for more than just a one gal show.

"Show me how you take care of yourself," he ordered.

Rolling onto my side, I started to reach for the nightstand where I had a small stim stashed. He grabbed my hips and moved me back. "No. Use your hand," he barked.

There was something about the way he was being so demanding that sent a throbbing pulsation between my legs. I fully relaxed on my back and slipped two fingers in my mouth to moisten them before moving my hand down toward my box. I ran my fingers along my pussy lips for a minute, occasionally slipping one or both inside me. Once my breathing started to quicken, I began rubbing my clit.

My head rolled back and I let the moans release that I normally keep contained when I take matters into my own hands. I switched to using my thumb on my clit, and I inserted both fingers inside me. With my head back and eyes closed, I wasn't watching to know that Lance was undressing at the side of the bed.

Lance grabbed my feet and yanked me toward the edge. My head jerked forward as I was suddenly dragged across the bed. He stood completely naked before me. His chest was well defined, and his muscles flexed with every move he made. I allowed my gaze to fall downward toward his waist until his stiff manhood came into view. I wanted to know how he felt, and I couldn't wait any longer.

I arched my back and lifted off the bed toward him, but he didn't move any closer. Lowering back down to the bed, I wrapped a foot around behind him and tried to nudge him to me.

"Is that all you want? Some quick fuck?" he asked me.

The truthful answer was yes. It didn't matter to me if it was hard and fast or slow and soft. As long as there was no mistake that this was only about sex and nothing more, he could have it anyway he wanted. I kept my foot wrapped around him, but I stopped trying to pull him to me with it. It wasn't easy coming up with an answer for him. This had to happen. I'd put so much time and energy into making sure I fucked him that I didn't want to risk saying the wrong thing and ruining it now.

"That's all she wants. It's like she only spreads her legs for me now because she feels like she has to from time to time in order to keep me content. That is until you showed up and made her feel like she had competition."

A slow smile spread across my face. So that's what this was about? He wanted something different than what his wife had been throwing his way all this time. I was more than willing to give him what he wanted.

I pulled my foot around and placed it on his chest, playfully pushing him back. "I think it's time for you to show me what you like," I said softly.

Lance took my foot in his hand

and rubbed it gently. He pulled it toward his face and gently sucked my toes into his mouth one by one. Then he kissed the inner part of my ankle and up my leg until he reached the top. Once he reached my inner thigh, he started over with my other foot.

The buildup was exciting. Normally, I'm not much for a lot of foreplay, but I've been working toward this moment for close to two months. Lance could take as long as he wanted tonight, and there'd be no complaints from me. If he wasn't already married, I'd think he was in it for the long haul with the way he so gently and lovingly took his time.

He bent forward over top of me

and traced his tongue from one nipple across my chest to the other one. Back and forth, he licked them and nibbled softly with his teeth. Soon he balanced himself on one hand and slipped the other between my legs, slowly rubbing my pussy lips and building speed. I felt two fingers slip inside me, and I started to moan.

Lance slid his arm under my back and pulled me close to him again, keeping his other hand stroking my box. His fingers thrust in and out until I was at the brink then he slipped his shaft inside me without removing his fingers. He used them to pull the opening of my pussy down and away to help ease his shockingly large cock all the way inside.

My moans were intensifying, and I thought he had finally fit his full length in my pussy. It didn't seem humanly possible there could be any more to him.

"You ready?" he asked breathlessly.

I looked him in the eye wondering what he could be meaning. He gave me a devilish smile before removing his fingers and wrapping his other arm underneath me as well. Holding me close to him, he thrust inside me forcefully while pulling my body toward him.

"Damn!" I cried out as his full cock entered me. It was the most cock I ever had in my pussy before, and I once took two dicks at a college party.

He paused and asked, "You okay?"

"Don't stop fucking me," I sneered at him.

His eyes lit up. He started thrusting in and out slowly while a constant stream of pussy juice ran down his cock and onto my bed. Every pump of his cock sent torrents of cum flowing. A low and steady stream of moans escaped my mouth while my eyes rolled back in my head.

"She has to take it slow and steady just like this or she can't handle it," he told me.

"Tonight... I'm yours," I told him between gasping breaths.

"However you want it."

He flashed that smile again and said, "I was hoping you would say that."

Lance moved his hands up under my back until they cupped my shoulders for a better grip. He started banging me hard and fast. Flashes of light appeared before my eyes, and I thought I might pass out. The pleasure was so intense. It was a struggle to keep my cries low enough to not wake the children.

After several minutes, he slowed down to check if I was okay again. It's considerate and all, but really ruins the mood when you're wanting a good fuck like that.

"Is there anything else she won't do for you?" I asked.

Lance opened his mouth to say something, but closed it without speaking. Then he shook his head no.

"There's lube in the nightstand," I told him.

His eyes widened, and he glanced at the nightstand. Turning back to me, he started pumping into me again building up speed.

"My ass is yours if you want it," I told him while I still had the breath to speak.

After a few more thrusts, he tore himself off me. Taking two steps to the drawer, he opened it and fished out the lube. "Roll over," he demanded.

I happily obliged, knowing I would probably regret this in the morning when my asshole pained me with every move I made.

He came up behind me, and I could hear him lubing up his cock. He fingered my ass and generously doused it with lube too. "No woman has ever let me come near her ass before," he told me.

"So I'm your first?" I giggled.

"Yes," he said, pushing the tip of his cock against my ass.

I relaxed as much as I could to prepare for Lance's massive size. The P.E. teacher tore me up without any lube except for my own cum, but his size paled by comparison.

I sucked in and held my breath as Lance pushed forward, and the knob of his dick penetrated my ass.

He tried to push forward, but was met with resistance from my tight hole. Pulling all the way out and trying again, he managed to penetrate further. He repeated it until he got into a steady fucking rhythm. My ass felt like it would burst, and I was certain he wasn't even all the way inside me.

As he worked his cock in and out of my ass, I buried my face into my sheets. I gripped the bedding with my hands and crumpled it up to my mouth to bite down on it for fear of moaning too loud and waking the children. Slowly in and out he went, and I orgasmed without having to play with my clit to encourage it. His size was massive enough that the pressure through the thin walls was all it took to stimulate my pussy while he fucked my ass.

Low moans started coming from him, and I knew he was getting close. Tears slowly rolled down my face from the painful pleasure he was eliciting in me, but I wanted him to have it all. I lifted my face from my bed for a moment, and ordered him, "Fuck me, Lance!"

There was no hesitation in his response. He grabbed my hips to steady me and began pounding my ass hard. I screamed into the sheets that were again gagging my mouth, but I pressed my ass back into him for more. Soon his bucking became jerky, and I knew his load was being shot inside me. He collapsed on top of me pressing me flat into the bed when he was done.

Before he shifted his weight and pulled out, he thanked me. It was odd. No one had ever thanked me for sex before, and I wasn't sure how I felt about it. He rolled me over and pressed his lips to mine. It was our first kiss. Also odd to think we'd had that much sex between us without something as simple as a kiss before.

He stood up and left the room telling me he'd be back. I thought he was going to clean up and maybe grab a glass of water. When he reappeared, he was in a robe. He pulled the sheet over me and carried me out of the room. I wondered what he had in store now, and I was surprised when he brought me to the master bath in his room. The water was running into a bubble filled tub. He set me in it, dropping the sheet to the floor as he did.

Lance turned the water off and told me to relax. He left the room and was gone for a while before returning. When he came back, he sat at the edge of the tub and slowly bathed me being very careful as he went. After my bath, he dried me off, wrapped me in a towel, and carried me back to my room where my bed was freshly made with clean sheets. He told me not to worry about a thing because he'd get the soiled ones out of the dryer and folded before Tori came home.

I lay in bed awake wondering how she could treat a man who was so caring the way she did. It also worried me that maybe Lance was beginning to see me as more than just a piece of ass. That's all I wanted. Well, I wanted to destroy their marriage, but by using sex to do it. It was time to leave. I needed to get out of this house and this job before I wind up breaking a heart in the process.

Chapter Nine

Dear Diary,

It's my last night working for the Rayburn's, only no one knows it but me. I decided to go out with a bang. Pun intended.

After taking the children to school, I made a stop for a job interview. Lance sleeps in since he works second shift, and Tori sleeps half the day away because she's a partying whore. I knew they wouldn't even notice I was late getting back.

The older man who owned the insurance office couldn't take his eyes off the slit in my dress except to stare at my cleavage. I knew the job was mine as soon as I walked in the door. Office experience? No. Computer savvy? Not really. Know anything about insurance? Not at all. Perfect! We'll train you. The administrative assistant job is mine as long as I can start right away. He wants me there first thing in the morning.

Driving back to the Rayburn's, I called my mom to let her know I'd be moving back that night. It wasn't working out. I found something else. Blah, blah, blah. It wasn't at all a lie, but it wasn't anything near the truth either.

They were both still in bed, so I grabbed a box that was destined for the recycle bin and put as much of my stuff as I could in it. I was able to get the box in my trunk before either of them left their room. I hadn't brought much with me to begin with, so all that was left was some clothes. I gathered everything and put it in my laundry basket. If they saw me carry it through the house, they'd just assume I was doing laundry. Tori might bitch since it's not my day off, and she'd claim I shouldn't be doing personal crap when I'm working. Since Lance was home, I'd have an ally.

I didn't bring it out of my room until it was time to pick the kids up, and neither of them saw me. Easy peasy. The only thing left to remove from the house was myself, but I wanted one last go with Lance first.

From spying on Tori's social media account, I knew she was going to a movie with a friend tonight. Legitimately not cheating for a change. The only thing more surprising is that she actually has friends. Lance wouldn't necessarily buy it. When you lie that much, you can't expect someone to believe you when you tell the truth. So yeah, she's claiming she's off to the movies, but as far as he knows, she's off to film a porno with five dudes she met at the gas station yesterday.

The point is that I know she'll be home relatively early while her husband won't expect her home until late. I did my research thoroughly. I knew what movie she was going to and how long it lasted. I also knew she told her friend she had to get home soon after it because if she didn't throw her husband a piece of ass from time to time, he might just start fucking the nanny. That made me laugh out loud. She'd find before too long just how right she was. I wanted to make sure we were in the heat of things when she got home. Like they say, hell hath no fury... That's me. I am woman scorned.

It'd been a few days since our last night together. I was definitely on the mend, but not sure I wanted round two in the ass just yet. Part of me thought it would be better if that's what his wife saw when she came home considering it was what she refused him.

As soon as I put the children to bed, I went to Lance's room and stripped down naked. I was only wearing a light dress and flip flops. I needed clothes that were easy to grab and put on as I ran from the house, presumably with an irate wife chasing after me. I laid across the bed and sent him a text message asking if he could help me with something upstairs.

Laying there, I listened for his footsteps coming up the stairs and down the hall. They stopped at my room, and I could tell he went inside expecting to find me there. Soon he made his way further down the hall to his bedroom and opened the door where I was waiting for him on the bed. I had the bottle of banana lube I stole from Tori in my hand fully anticipating using it on Lance, and another bottle of lube for my ass nearby just in case.

As soon as he saw me, he practically leapt at the bed. He began kissing me while fumbling to take off his sweats. He traced kisses down my neck and across my breasts. Once he was naked, I ordered him to sit on the bed, and he did as instructed.

I gobbed the lube over his cock and began eating my dessert. I have never been one to shy away from giving a blow job, but this lube was unbelievable. It tasted amazing and made my enthusiasm that much more heightened. I was on a roll lapping up every last drop as I feveriishly bobbed up and down on his cock that I was truly disappointed when he pushed me away saying he didn't want to come yet.

Lance stood up and laid me back on the bed. He knelt between my legs and cupped his hands around my legs on my ass. He began by kissing my inner thighs and slowly moved to my pussy where he worked the outer lips before penetrating me with his tongue. I groaned and bucked up into his face.

He lifted his head back and tilted it to the side giving me a weird look. Could it be he's never had a woman fuck his face before?

"What was that?" he asked.

I grinned from ear to ear. "Another first, huh? You are in for a real treat."

Without another word, he went back to tonguing me while playing with my clit. I grabbed his head and started grinding into his face hard.

He pulled back again to say, "Damn! I like that," but before he could finish speaking, I pulled his head back to my crotch to fuck his face harder.

After several orgasms, I eased up on him, and he shifted to slip his cock inside me. I put my hand on his chest and gently pushed him back. "No, I want to be on top," I told him.

I saw the disappointment on his face. He had confided in me a couple days ago that his wife is always on top so she can control how much of him she takes because she can't handle all of him. "Trust me," I said. "Just for a bit."

He laid back on the bed and let me climb on top of him. I slowly eased myself down on his cock until he was fully inside me. I smiled at him mischievously because I knew that was the reason he was leery about this position. He wanted full penetration, but wasn't used to getting it. I always give what my man of the night wants. He placed his hands on my hips and groaned. I started riding him slowly. His cock was a lot to take, and I needed to build up gradually.

I glanced quickly at the clock and saw we had about fifteen minutes before the earliest I expected Tori to be home, and that's if she drove straight home from the theater after the movie ended. There was enough time for me to be fully satisfied before we were caught.

Bit by bit, I increased my speed until I was riding him hard. My lip bled from biting it so hard to prevent loud moans coming from my mouth. When the pain in my lip got too severe, I bit the other side until it bled too. Orgasm after orgasm washed over me. I felt flushed and warm. My legs shook uncontrollably next to his hips.

Lance gently squeezed my hips and said, "Let's switch. I think you're about wore out."

I looked him in the eyes and said, "Oh, no. I'm not done yet."

Reaching under the blanket near us, I pulled out the bottle of anal lube. "I want to ride you with your cock in my ass," I told him.

The sound of his breath sucking through his teeth was loud and clear. I'm surprised the excitement of hearing me say it alone wasn't enough to push him over the edge to cum. I rolled to the side and lifted off of him, handing him the lube. As he worked on lubing up his cock, I turned him around to ride him reverse.

He positioned one hand on my hip and the other on his shaft to help guide him into my ass. My hole cried out as soon as the tip touched it, begging not to be violated again so soon. I pushed through the objections from my body, and once his cock was about halfway inside, the pain lessoned, being replaced with almost pure pleasure.

Facing away from him, I kept my eyes on the closed bedroom door without him seeing where my attention was focused. I raised and lowered myself on his cock slowly. Each time I came down, I took a little more of his length inside. Steady moans rolled from my mouth, and I tried to stay as quiet as I could. My lips were too damaged to keep biting on them. My dress was laying on the edge of the bed, and I grabbed it to cork my mouth. It was perfect since I'd need to grab it in a hurry once Tori showed up anyway.

Once I was gagged again, I started to build my tempo. My ass began to blaze with pain once more as I took in more and more of his cock. Finally, I felt my ass touch his abdomen and couldn't believe I fit so much inside. I leaned forward more and started bucking into him to allow him to go even deeper. Once I got used to his length, I started to pick up speed.

"Vicki…" he moaned. "Oh my god, Vicki."

I kept riding and grinding into him faster and faster. His cock was splitting my ass open, but I didn't care. Cum streamed out of me and washed over his balls.

"Oh, fuck, woman!" he cried, and I knew he was getting close.

I started to worry that my timing would be off. That maybe Tori would get home later than I expected her, and we'd be over and cleaned up before she showed. It was my last night in this house no matter what, and I'd be leaving with the fuck of my life. Still, I wanted her to catch me. To catch us. I wanted her to see me, the useless nanny that she treated like crap because she thought I was beneath her, riding her husband with his cock in my ass. In her bed of all places to add insult to injury. Not that she really had any room to say shit given her constant indiscretions, but I wanted to do all the damage I could. Now, here was Lance on the verge of release, and his wife was nowhere in sight.

"Vicki…Vicki," he kept repeating. His voice grew louder each time he said my name.

At last, the doorknob on the bedroom door started to turn very slowly. Tori had to have heard him crying out my name in the hall. He was the one being too loud now, and the way she was slowly turning the knob told me she didn't want to give us a chance to roll over and cover up before walking in the room.

Looking away from the door, I gave it everything I had and rode his cock like my life depended on it. I let the dress fall from my mouth and cried out, "Yes, Lance. Fuck my tight ass! Harder!" There would be no mistake for Tori about exactly what we were doing.

Lance started bucking and jerking below me. His hot stream of cum warmed me up from the inside.

"Damn, Vicki!" he almost yelled. "Your ass is amazing! Fuuuuucccckkkk!"

From the corner of my eye, I could see the open door as his release ended, and his body relaxed. The timing couldn't be more perfect. Tori was getting quite the eye and earful.

"I fucking love you," Lance let slip out plain as day.

That was an added bonus. I had suspected there might be feelings involved, but I would never have expected the "L" word so soon, and definitely not in front of his wife.

"What the actual fuck?!" Tori screamed from the doorway.

I rolled to the side, allowing Lance's cock to ease out of my ass. Holding my dress in front of my nude body, I pretended to be shocked to see her there.

"You fucking slut!" Tori screamed at me and lunged in my direction.

Lance moved between us, and

she pelted his chest with her tiny fists until he grabbed her wrists to stop her.

I pulled my dress over my head, slipping it on as fast as I could then grabbed my shoes to carry as I ran out of the house. Flip flops weren't the best shoes to wear when running from a married woman on a mission. Moving around the bed toward the door, I kept my eyes on Tori in case she broke free from Lance's hold.

Tori just uttered a stream of obscenities in my direction, calling me every name she could think to say. "What do you have to say for yourself, you home wrecking whore?" she yelled as I made it past her.

Seriously? Every man in town has probably had her at least once. The looks and sly smirks I see when people hear the name of the family I work for tell me that no one in town is oblivious to her running around on her husband. Yet, I'm the homewrecker?

"Honestly, I didn't think you'd care considering you've sucked every dick in town at least once," I spat back.

"Vicki!" It was Lance this time. The surprise from what I said caused him to loosen his grip, and Tori made a move.

I bolted from the room feeling her finger tips barely graze my ponytail. There was a loud thud behind me, and I knew without looking back that she lost her balance and fell.

"I'm going to kill you, you fucking bitch!" I heard her scream as I ran down the stairs.

I ran outside and got in my car. Once I realized she wasn't coming out after me, I started laughing. Putting the car in reverse, I backed out and peeled out into the street. There was no way I was giving her a chance to catch up to me.

I smiled as I watch their house disappear in the rear view mirror. Even the throbbing from my wrecked ass couldn't knock the smirk off my face at that point. There's something about a plan coming together perfectly that makes everything else seem alright.

Coming Soon

Nanny Diaries #3

Mindy Cummings didn't except anything from Mark Jacobs expect a decent paying part time nanny job that worked well with her college schedule. The apartment over the garage for her own private affairs was an added bonus. She soon learned how little she knew about the man she'd been babysitting for since she was a teen. It wouldn't take long to realize that his touch was the one thing she needed more than anything.

Fantasy after fantasy, he filled her thoughts. His face was who she envisioned no matter who she was with. The one thing she didn't expect was for fantasy to become reality.

More by Darling Coxx

Nanny Diaries #1

Lacey Moore bit off more than she could swallow when she took the position at the Wyndham estate. What was supposed to be the perfect job accompanied by great hours, pay and perks like living rent free in the guest house soon turned out to be more than she had could have ever imagined. The main duties of her job included making sure the entire staff stayed satisfied, and it was a job she intended on doing well.

Nanny Diaries #2

Vicki Sweet didn't know what she was walking into when she took the job as nanny for the Rayburn's. Soon she found herself loaded with maid duties as well as chasing after the children while Lance worked and ignored all of his wife's illicit activities. Tori Rayburn needed to be put in her place, and Vicki was just the woman for the job. Chasing after Tori's affairs, Vicki began stealing them away one by one, but her eye remained on the ultimate prize. Vicki would have her saucy way with Lance before her job ended, and once she set her mind

on something, she always got what
she wanted.

About the Author

Darling Coxx is a seasoned writer who has been featured in many major publications under her given name. Taking a break from interviews and personal experience pieces, she is trying her hand at short novellas in the same genre she's been working in for most of her life.

Her adult entertainment career began while working as the manager of an adult store. It is her favorite position of any she's held, before or since. It was there where she made the contacts that allowed her to venture into the world of adult entertainment both in her own writing as well as producing a few pieces of her own.

Please feel free to reach out to her at DarlingCoxx@gmail.com. Follow her on Instagram @DarlingCoxx to stay updated on future publications. And don't forget to subscribe to her OnlyFans account @DarlingCoxx.